SPARKY

This is the gay story, told in both text and spirited pictures, of an imaginative little trolley car who somehow cannot keep his mind on his work. In his colorful adventures, the artist-author has recaptured the irresistible charm which has made his *Little Toot* a beloved classic with readers of all ages.

ALL ABOARD!

SPARKY

The Story of a Little Trolley Car

Story and Pictures by

HARDIE GRAMATKY

G. P. Putnam's Sons · New York

SPARKY is a bustling little trolley car who goes back and forth a dozen times a day between the Town Square and the Picnic Grounds out where the open country meets the edge of town. Sparky wakes up early every morning at the carbarn where he sleeps. It is his job to take the grownups in to work and home again at night. Busy, cheerful, helpful, Sparky is an important member of the community. He likes the people along his route. They like Sparky and listen for the sound of his bell. He is proud of his bright red and yellow paint-job and of his name which is neatly painted on each side.

Sparky's life would not be very exciting, going back and forth along the same streets every day, seeing the same store fronts and the same houses, if Sparky were an ordinary trolley car. Luckily for him, he has a wonderful imagination. When his busy little mind is at work, sparks fly from his trolley, and you know that he is up to something.

When he passes the barber shop down near the Square, he likes to think that the barber pole is a stick of peppermint candy. He can picture the high old time his young friends would have, if it really were something to eat.

When Sparky hears a train whistle, he may forget all about what he is doing and start imagining that he is traveling to far places as the caboose on a rumbling freight. When he splashes through the puddles after a heavy rain, it makes him think of being a speedboat, throwing up white plumes of spray as he roars across the water. If he hears the sound of a lively march as he passes the Music Store, Sparky has no trouble at all thinking of a parade. That is what he likes best of all to dream about—the excitement of the crowd as the parade passes by with Sparky proudly out in front leading the band.

Down near the center of town, Sparky passes the window of the Big Store. One morning when Sparky saw himself in the window, he gave a sudden start and his sparks fairly flew. There was a new Sparky— sleek and long and streamlined, like the engine of a fast train.

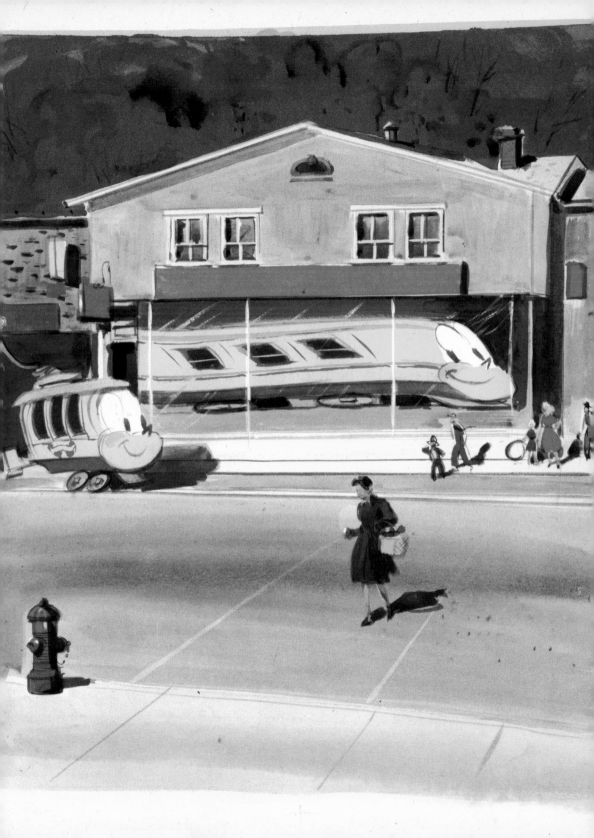

Then Sparky caught a glimpse of his reflection in the window of the Butcher Shop. He looked fat and round like a sausage. It brought him back to earth.

It was high time, too, because Sparky was almost at the Town Square. As he went by the Town Hall, the Fire House, and the Post Office, he had to move carefully through the crowds of people all dressed in their Sunday best. Flags were waving, and the band was playing. The Mayor was just driving up in his handsome old sports car with its shiny brass headlights. The benches had been set up in front of the speakers' stand; there were going to be speeches, and Sparky was going to lead the parade.

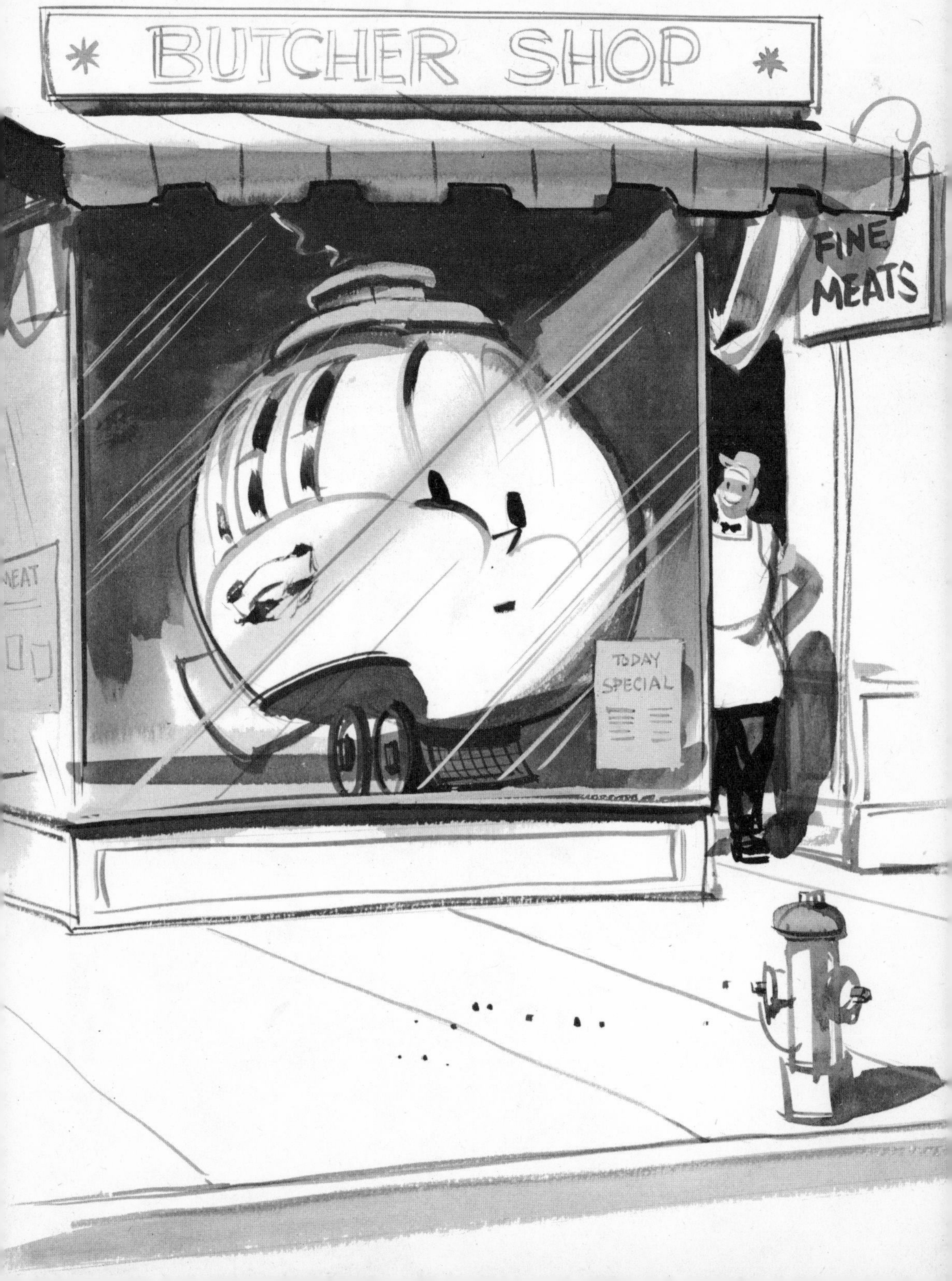
BUTCHER SHOP
FINE MEATS
TODAY SPECIAL
MEAT

Sparky dreamed about the parade and the gay music of the band all the rest of the day. The next morning, when he started in toward town, he was still thinking what a wonderful time he had had. Way up ahead, he could see the crowd gathering at his stop, and that was all Sparky's imagination needed. Sparky fancied that he could hear music and people cheering. He imagined he was still leading the parade, beating time with his trolley.

Sparks were flying as he scooted along. He imagined the crowd was cheering the leader of the band and he forgot to stop. The people jumped and shouted and some of them ran after him. The noise finally woke Sparky from his dream and he remembered where he was. He had just pulled up, when the Mayor stopped his car right beside him.

The Mayor was furious and saw a chance to show off in front of the crowd. He got out of his car and shook his finger in Sparky's face. He raged and shouted. He tweaked Sparky's nose and snapped his trolley up and down. The people were a little ashamed of the Mayor and felt sorry for Sparky.

The Mayor told the Town Council about Sparky's running past his stop, and he even suggested doing away with Sparky entirely.

"We could make Sparky into a diner, if he doesn't behave," said the Mayor.

When Sparky was told what might happen to him, he was horrified. He shuddered every time he thought of it.

Imagine being made into a diner!

The hardest part of Sparky's route between the Town Square and the Picnic Grounds is up the steep hill. Even with a good start, Sparky is puffing and shooting sparks when he reaches the top. At the foot of the hill is a neat little house with a white picket fence. This is where Jimmie lives. Jimmie is four years old and is one of Sparky's best friends.

Jimmie always waves to Sparky from his front gate. Sparky waves his trolley in return. The friendly exchange seems to give Sparky just the help he needs to make the top of the hill.

The part of Sparky's route that he doesn't like runs past the Old House at the top of the hill. Set back from the street, the Old House is falling to pieces.

Passing the Old House in the daytime, you can see what it really looks like. Sparky knows that there is nothing to be afraid of in the dark, but when he is scurrying by the Old House at night, he sometimes forgets. He is glad he doesn't have to stop there then.

Sparky is always happy when he comes to the bridge over the creek out at the Picnic Grounds.

On bright sunny afternoons, the fishermen look up with a smile and say:

"Here comes Sparky."

Sometimes Sparky helps by reaching way down with his trolley if a big pickerel is hooked near the bridge.

One day when Sparky went by the Post Office, he saw a helicopter landing with mail on the roof. Sparks started to fly, and you could tell that Sparky's imagination was busy again. Sparky began to think how wonderful it would be to fly, with his trolley whirling above him. He could just see himself soaring above the crowds.

If I could just swing my trolley all the way around, thought Sparky, I know I could fly. Sparky couldn't wait. He had to try it.

He gave his trolley an extra hard swing, and around it went, slowly at first, and then faster and faster. But the faster he spun his trolley, the dizzier Sparky became. All of a sudden, his front wheels slipped off the track and there was Sparky sprawling like a puppy right in the middle of traffic.

There was quite a hullabaloo. . . .

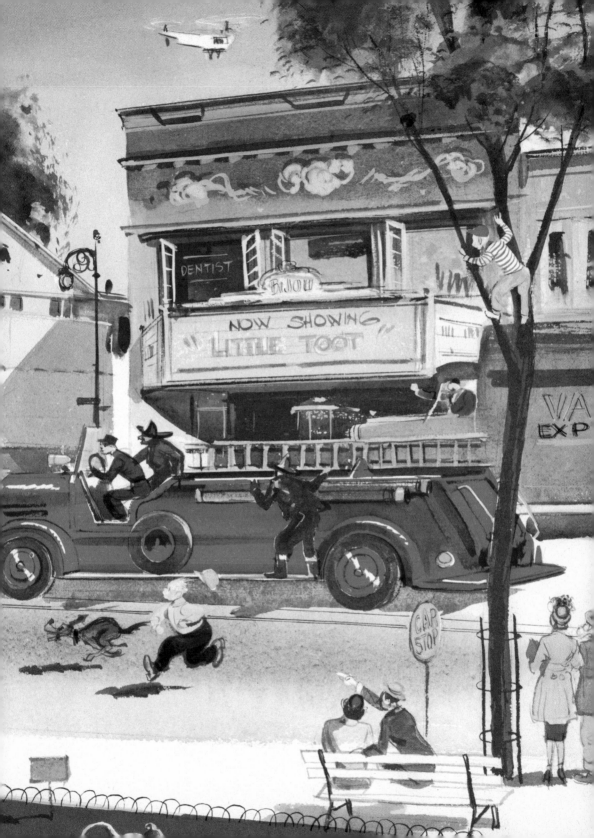

"If you do anything like this again," the Mayor told Sparky, "you *will* be made into a diner."

Sparky shivered to think of being a diner in the wintertime. He would be out all night in the snow and wind with no warm carbarn to sleep in. Sparky decided to behave.

During the next few days, Sparky did behave, and he was very helpful. He rescued a frightened kitten that had climbed into a tree and couldn't get down.

He stopped a baby carriage halfway down the steep hill.

Sparky was working hard and he was trying to be serious. Back and forth he went from the Town Square to the Picnic Grounds a dozen times a day. He rang his bell politely if people were in the way, and he waved to his special friend, Jimmie, each time he started up the hill.

One afternoon when Sparky passed the sand lot where the boys were playing ball, he almost forgot himself again. He could imagine himself as a famous ballplayer hitting the homer that would save the pennant. But thinking of baseball made him think of hot dogs, and hot dogs made him think of a diner. That was all the warning Sparky needed. Without even stopping, he scooted off toward town.

Late that afternoon, Sparky missed Jimmie at the bottom of the hill. Jimmie wanted to find out where his friend Sparky went and he had decided to hide as Sparky passed and then follow him.

Jimmie knew that he was supposed to ask his mother if he could leave the yard. He also was pretty sure that, if he told his mother he was going after Sparky, she would say no. So Jimmie took his red wagon and started up the hill without saying anything.

Jimmie trudged on up the hill until he came to the Old House. When he saw the open gates, he *had* to go exploring inside.

It was getting on toward dark when Sparky came back to the Old House, and he could see the long shadows reaching out for him. Sparks were flying as he put on speed to scamper past. Then out of the corner of his eye, he caught a glimpse of something red. It was Jimmie's wagon. Jimmie must be inside.

It was one of the hardest things Sparky had ever had to do. He pulled up right there in front of the Old House where he had never dared stop before. There was Jimmie.

Sparky clanged his bell, and Jimmie eagerly climbed aboard. Off went Sparky down the hill to Jimmie's house as fast as he could go.

Sparky slid to a stop right in the middle of the block in front of Jimmie's house. Jimmie had no sooner jumped off into his anxious mother's arms than—*bang, crash, thump*—something hit Sparky from behind. Then above the tinkling sound of falling glass, Sparky heard a voice he knew only too well. It belonged to the Mayor, and the Mayor was fit to be tied. He had driven his old car right into Sparky's back platform.

Sparky hadn't been damaged at all. Where it hurt was inside; and Sparky's spirits drooped lower and lower as the Mayor stamped and ranted. Sparky knew that this time the Mayor would carry out his threat to make him into a diner, and the full indignity of being put out of service suddenly became very real. They would take off his cowcatcher; they would hang a heavy sign on his trolley; they would remove his precious steps. Worst of all, they would paint over his name which was so neatly lettered on each side. Sparky could see it all happening.

At the next meeting of the Town Council, the Mayor was still angry.

"Sparky is through," he said. "We'll make him into a diner. We'll tear down the Old House and put him way out there."

The Councilmen all voted YES.

The news of Sparky's fate spread like ripples on a pond. Poor Sparky himself had never felt so downhearted. It would be bad enough to be made into a diner, but to be put out there alone on the top of the hill in place of the Old House really scared him. He went right on working, and his load seemed to be getting bigger and bigger.

It was the afternoon of Sparky's last run that the Mayor chose to drive out to the Old House. He wanted to find out what had to be done. The Mayor was in a hurry as usual. He jumped out of his car at the top of the steep hill and rushed past the rusty iron gates.

Now the Mayor's car was feeling as old as it looked. It was simply worn out, and running into Sparky hadn't helped a bit. Even with its front straightened out and its headlights back in place, it ached in every joint. When the Mayor left it on the hill, the car gripped its brakes as tightly as it could. It groaned and dug its tires into the pavement; it strained every nut and bolt. It was touch and go whether it could hold on or not.

The Mayor glanced around just in time to see his car start slipping slowly backward. Then it went plunging down the hill, faster and faster, with the Mayor in full cry after it.

Down at the bottom of the hill, Jimmie and the neighbors were waiting to say good-by to Sparky on his last trip.

Sparky saw Jimmie, as he came up. Then he heard the Mayor shouting and saw the Mayor's car. Sparky was the first to realize what was happening. His wheels churned. Sparks flew as he put on every ounce of power. It was as brave an act as you will ever see—Sparky, heedless of his own danger, dashing to the rescue.

Sparky was not a second too soon. . . .

When it was over, Jimmie's mother couldn't thank Sparky enough. The neighbors who had seen it all happen turned on the Mayor and, this time, placed the blame where it belonged.

The Mayor apologized. He admitted that it was all his fault for leaving his old car on the hill where its brakes couldn't hold. He was genuinely sorry about Sparky.

So, in the end, Sparky was a hero.

The people all said they knew that they could never get along without Sparky. He was as much a part of the town as they were themselves. Even the Mayor became his friend and declared a "Sparky Day."

Now, every year, they celebrate. And Sparky leads the parade, beating time with his trolley.

SPARKY'S
DAILY RUN